# little Miss Neat

## by Roger Hargreaves

**PSS!**
PRICE STERN SLOAN
An Imprint of Penguin Group (USA) Inc.

Little Miss Neat was a very tidy person.

Probably the tidiest person in the whole world.

She lived in Twopin Cottage.

It was called Twopin Cottage because she kept it as neat as two pins!

She just couldn't stand a mess.

Every day she spent all day polishing and dusting and cleaning and making sure that things were in their proper places.

One morning, Little Miss Neat awoke in her bedroom at Twopin Cottage.

She looked out of her bedroom window.

It had been raining during the night, and there was a puddle in the middle of her garden path.

"Oh," she gasped in horror, and rushed outside with a dust cloth.

She mopped up every drop of puddle, and then she rushed inside and washed the dust cloth, and then she ironed the dust cloth, and then she folded the dust cloth, and then she placed the dust cloth very neatly back in its drawer.

Everything in Twopin Cottage had its proper place!

Now, this story is about the time Little Miss Neat went on vacation.

She always went away for one week every summer, and this year was no different.

She spent two days packing.

And then she spent a whole day polishing her suitcase.

And then off she set, leaving Twopin Cottage all neat and tidy.

"Oh, I hope it doesn't get too dusty while I'm away," she thought as she closed the door behind her.

But something worse than dusty was going to happen to Twopin Cottage.

Would you like to know what?

Mr. Muddle came to tea!

He'd written to Miss Neat to tell her, but being Mr. Muddle, he somehow got into a muddle mailing the letter.

Actually, what happened was that when Mr. Muddle went to mail the letter, he had the letter in one hand and a half-eaten sandwich in the other.

And you can guess what happened, can't you?

That's right!

He mailed the sandwich!

"It'll be nice seeing Miss Neat again," he chuckled to himself as he walked home. "This sandwich is a bit chewy," he thought.

It was the day after Miss Neat left that Mr. Muddle arrived.

He walked up the garden path of Twopin Cottage and knocked at the door.

No reply!

"Good-bye!" he shouted.

It should have been "Hello!" but he isn't called Mr. Muddle for nothing.

"Nobody home?" he called.

He pushed open the door.

"Oh dear," he thought as he looked around. "Nobody home!"

"Never mind," he thought. "I'll make myself a cup of tea and wait for Miss Neat."

So he went into the kitchen of Twopin Cottage, made himself a cup of tea, and waited.

And waited.

And waited.

And waited.

And went home.

Little Miss Neat stepped out of the taxi at Twopin Cottage.

"That was a lovely vacation," she said, paying the taxi driver. "But it's nice to be home."

She walked up the garden path, and went in through the door.

"Not too dusty," she said to herself looking around. "I think I'll make myself a nice cup of tea before I start unpacking."

But, making tea after a Mr. Muddle visit isn't quite as easy as it sounds.

Little Miss Neat eventually found the teapot.

Not in its proper place.

In the refrigerator!

And she eventually found the milk.

Not in its proper place.

In the teapot!

And the tea.

In the sugar bowl!

And the sugar.

In the milk jug!

And a cup.

In the oven!

And a saucer.

In the breadbox!

But could she find a teaspoon?

She could not!

The telephone rang.

Little Miss Neat picked it up.

"Hello," she said.

At the other end of the line, Mr. Muddle suddenly realized he was holding the telephone the wrong way.

He turned it the right way.

"Good-bye," he said.

"Who's that?" asked Miss Neat.

"It's you," replied Mr. Muddle.

Miss Neat thought.

"It's Mr. Muddle, isn't it?" she guessed.

"Yes," replied Mr. Muddle, getting it right for once.

"And you paid me a visit while I was away on vacation, didn't you?" she guessed again.

"Yes," replied Mr. Muddle, getting it right twice. "Can I come and see you now that you're back?"

"I suppose so," sighed Miss Neat. "Good-bye!"

"Hello!" said Mr. Muddle.

And put the phone down.

Little Miss Neat sighed a heavy sigh and sat down in the armchair next to the telephone.

Ouch!!

She looked underneath the cushion.

There were all her teaspoons.

And knives!

And forks!

I don't think Little Miss Neat will be taking a vacation next year.

Do you?